I0646328

THE INNKEEPER'S WIFE

THE REST OF
THE CHRISTMAS STORY

WRITTEN BY

LYNDA M. WILSON

ILLUSTRATED BY

BRANDON DORMAN

SHADOW
MOUNTAIN

Text © 2006 Lynda M. Wilson

Illustrations © 2006 Brandon Dorman

Design by Meridith Ethington

All rights reserved. No part of this book may be reproduced in any form or by any means without permission in writing from the publisher, Shadow Mountain®. The views expressed herein are the responsibility of the author and do not necessarily represent the position of Shadow Mountain.

Visit us at shadowmountain.com

Library of Congress Cataloging-in-Publication Data

Wilson, Lynda M.
   The innkeeper's wife / Lynda M. Wilson.
     p.   cm.
   ISBN 10- 1-59038-479-2 (alk. paper)
   ISBN 13- 978-1-59038-479-4 (alk. paper)
   1. Luke, Saint—Fiction.   2. Christian saints—Fiction.   3. Evangelists (Bible)—Fiction.   4. Jesus Christ—Nativity—Fiction.   I. Title.
   PS3623.I58554I56   2005
   813'.6—dc22   2005015967

Printed in Mexico
R. R. Donnelley and Sons, Reynosa, Mexico

10 9 8 7 6 5 4 3 2

Dedication

TO SALLIE AND TERESA
MY ANGELS, WHO TAUGHT ME THAT
THE LORD SENDS HANNAHS
—LW

TO EVERYONE WHO LOVES
THE CHRIST CHILD STORY
—BD

CONTENTS

Chapter One THE MEETING

PAGE 1

Chapter Two THE BIRTH

PAGE 7

Chapter Three THE BABY

PAGE 19

Chapter Four THE SHEPHERDS

PAGE 23

Chapter Five THE PROMISE

PAGE 35

Oh, come, all ye faithful,

Joyful and triumphant!

Oh, come ye, oh, come ye to Bethlehem.

Come and behold him,

Born the King of angels;

Oh, come, let us adore him,

Christ, the Lord.

JOHN F. WADE; TRANSLATED BY FREDERICK OAKELEY

Chapter One

THE MEETING

The old woman and the traveler stood in the courtyard of Bethlehem's only inn, looking at one another. At a glance, one would have had the impression that they had been turned to statues by the heavy heat of the afternoon and the weariness that seemed to hang about each of them. But in fact they were studying one another closely.

The traveler made mental note of the unruly froth of white hair framing the part of the woman's weathered face that had escaped a hastily thrown-on shawl. On her cheek he saw the heavy creases of sound sleep. He knew she would be annoyed at having been awakened from an afternoon nap. Yet the map of years written on her face revealed a woman who had smiled much more often than she had frowned. Her gray eyes were mild, and the man took hope. The whole reason he had come was to gain this woman's trust.

For her part, the woman saw a traveler with at least three days of road dust upon him. Sweat from the hot sun had run down his face, drawing upon it another map, a smeared writing of heat and toil. His clothes showed him to be a foreigner, plainly dressed without either ostentation or sign of poverty. She wondered that he would come so far by himself. But most of all she wondered why he had insisted that her grandchildren wake her. He had asked specifically to speak with the innkeeper's wife—"the old one."

"Forgive me. I know you're busy," he said courteously, for it was obvious to him that the old woman's role in the inn had long ceased to be a very active one. "I don't wish to waste your time, but I think you may be able to help me."

"Do you seek lodging?"

"No. I have traveled with friends who have gone on to Jerusalem. It is you I wish to see."

"You seem to know who I am, sir. Who are you?"

"Forgive me. My name is Luke. I come from Philippi in Macedonia. I have friends who said you might remember something that happened here nearly forty years ago."

"You are a long way from home, Master Luke. Who are these friends that sent you to me?"

"A man named Simon Peter and his brother Andrew—from Capernaum in Galilee. They said that the innkeeper's wife would know—"

She held up her hand to stop him.

"You want to know about the night the baby was born, the one called Jesus of Nazareth?"

Luke nodded.

"Are you a follower of his?"

"I am."

"My name is Hannah. So am I."

Hannah offered Luke a seat in the canopied shade beside the courtyard wall. She brought him water and a towel, then dates and goat's milk.

Luke accepted these ministrations gratefully. Then, once these necessary matters of hospitality were accomplished, the woman began to speak.

O little town of Bethlehem,

How still we see thee lie.

Above thy deep and dreamless sleep

The silent stars go by;

Yet in thy dark streets shineth

The everlasting Light.

The hopes and fears of all the years

Are met in thee tonight.

PHILLIPS BROOKS

Chapter Two

THE BIRTH

There was indeed an unusual birth here in Bethlehem, at the time of Caesar's census, more than thirty-five years ago. My part in it was very small, but I have always been grateful that God granted me such a favor—to be able to help them.

"I remember it very well. My husband, Nathan, was the keeper of the inn then. My son, Jonah, is innkeeper now.

"When we heard the decree of Rome that every Judean must return to his ancestral home, we knew it would mean a windfall for us. Bethlehem is the city of King David. She had many sons and daughters who would have to return here to have their names taken. This small inn in such a small city does not normally have reason to do such business. At Passover we are busy; but this was as two Passovers—no, ten Passovers.

"In fact, we were overwhelmed. The city overflowed with travelers. The crowds meant that all of us were very busy. We put up tents in the field beyond this wall to make more room. We let our friends sell animal feed and goods from booths in the street there. We were running from morning to night. But I'm not complaining. We made money, and it was good to see old friends among those who returned. The weather was mild—it was the first month of the new year.[1]

---

[1] The first month of the Jewish year is Nissan, which corresponds to our late March—early April.

"The only real problem was space. We had squeezed every soul into the inn, its courtyard, and the tents who could possibly be squeezed in. We sent others to those in the town willing to open their homes for a fee. Bethlehem was bursting at its seams that day.

"The afternoon was drawing on when my son, who was ten or eleven at that time, came running, 'Look, Mother! More travelers. I followed them down the road from Simon's fields. I told the man to come here.'

"My son, Jonah, had been hired out to help Simon, a shepherd, during lambing season. I certainly did not need him scouring the roads around Bethlehem for more people to send to our already crowded inn. I turned to look at these additional people, annoyed at my son, annoyed at them.

"I saw the man talking with my husband. His wife sat on a donkey, next to him. The poor girl; I saw at once that she was with child, and far along, too.

"She looked so weary from her journey. She was young, and as they had no others with them I thought to myself, *This must be her first baby.*

"I saw Nathan pointing up the hill. I watched as they walked away. I also saw the girl's face. It was obvious to me that her discomfort was great.

"I ran to my husband. 'What did you say to them? Where did you send them? Didn't you see the condition of his wife?'

"He must have thought a magpie had swooped down on him. 'Hannah, Hannah. What could I say to them? I had to tell them the truth—that there is no room in the inn. Is

there a spot of ground in this whole courtyard not covered by man or beast?! Will you turn us out of our own beds?'

"He was right of course. Nathan had as good a heart as any man—better—but there really was no place to put them. Nathan had advised them to go to Matthias, a farmer on the edge of town. But he had sent others there already. As I watched them trudge wearily up the road, I hoped there would be room for this man and his wife.

"I was busy enough with the tasks at hand, it's true . . . but I could not forget them. Finally I called my son.

"'Jonah, follow them. I want to know if Matthias had room for them.'

"The afternoon was turning late when he returned.

"'No,' he reported, 'there was no room at Matthias's house.' But they had come back into town at the farmer's suggestion to try Beulah, the priest's widow.

"'And was there room for them there?' I demanded.

"'I don't think so. The man helped the lady off their donkey, and they are sitting under the palms at the well, eating their dinner.'

"They were not the only ones wanting food. Dinnertime was the busiest time of my day, and all around me were hungry people needing to be served. Finally things began to quiet down. Our guests were laying out their mats, settling their children, taking care of their animals. I should have been able to sit a moment. But I could not rest.

"Finally, I looked up to heaven. 'She needs me, doesn't she?' I whispered to the sky. It was not really a question, you know. My heart already had its answer.

"I explained to my husband. 'Nathan, I'm going out. I'm going to look for them. I have to know if that girl is all right.' I took a lantern and hastened into the darkness.

"He didn't try to stop me. I knew he was worried about them as well. Just as I was leaving, he called to me. 'Hannah, if you find them, tell them they can stay tonight in the far stable.'

"Three furlongs away was a small cave we used for our own animals when the inn was full. Yes—it would be just the right place. It had been cleaned only two days before and new straw put down. And it was sheltered, out of the wind, and private.

"I ran toward the center of town, my only thought to find the young couple. That turned out to be easy. They had not moved from their spot near the well, where my son had last seen them. The young woman was leaning her back against the kneeling donkey's flank. Her head resting on her husband's shoulder, and I thought for a moment that she might be crying. When I approached, her young husband jumped up and stood between us. 'Who's there?' he cried out.

"I held up the lantern and she looked up, pale in the light, but not crying. She was certainly beautiful.

"Poor fellow. How helpless he must have felt. All he wanted to do in the whole world was take care of her.

"'I'm the innkeeper's wife. My name is Hannah. There was no place to go, then, in the town?'

"'No place,' he said simply.

"'Then come with me. My husband says you can stay the night in our stable. It is a little way from the inn, but I think you will be all right there.'

"The young man looked at his wife and waited. 'Yes, Joseph. We can't stay here.' Suddenly her face tightened, and she reached for her husband's hand. She put her head down, and all she said was, 'Oh!'

"That was all the incentive I needed. I saw instantly that her husband, though he would have defended her at that moment with his very life, could not help her. His wife was in labor.

"She was very young. She needed her mother. She needed her mother's friends and the midwife of her village. This was certainly a cruel trick that fate and Caesar Augustus had played on them. She had none of the help she should have had.

"But she had me. I moved to her side and helped her to her feet.

"'Come quickly. I can help you.'

"She looked right into my eyes. She looked for a long moment as if she were waiting for something. Then she smiled at me.

"'Thank you,' she said. 'I knew his Father would send someone to help us.'

"Now wasn't that an odd thing to say? Well . . . Joseph and I got Mary—that was the young woman's name—to the stable. I kept my arm around her shoulders while Joseph made a bed for her on the straw and put his cloak on it. When she was as comfortable as I could make her, I turned to leave. I was going to need to get some things from the inn—towels, salt, oil.

"'Oh, Hannah, please don't leave me,' she begged, her voice frightened.

"'I'll be back, Mary. I won't be gone but a moment.'

"I raced to the inn. As I grabbed the things I would need, I explained to Nathan what I was doing.

"'God go with you,' he said to me. And He *was* with me. All went well."

Chapter Three

THE BABY

annah!" Luke stopped her. "Is that all you have to tell me of his birth—that it went well?"

She laughed. "You're a man, Luke. And men always think the birth of a baby to be a great mystery. I assure you it's a lot more work than mystery. No matter who it is who's being born, it takes many hours of work before the little one can take his first breath. But I had been at many births before. I knew how to help her. What I had to offer was enough.

"Look up there. Can you see behind that grove of palms, where the path bends behind the big rock? The stable where he was born is in a cave just beyond there. Before you leave you must walk up and see the place.

"Of course, none of us that night cared that we were in a stable. We were just thankful that both mother and baby were all right. God be praised.

"He was a beautiful, healthy baby boy. Joseph just kept saying 'Thank you' and 'God bless you,' over and over. I have a feeling he was thinking about what the night might have been like if I hadn't been there."

Hannah laughed again. Watching her, Luke felt the unashamed flush of her pride. He did not bother to tell her that he himself was a doctor and had attended many births. But, still, he found himself envying her this one.

Silent night! Holy night!

All is calm, all is bright

Round yon virgin mother and Child.

Holy Infant, so tender and mild,

Sleep in heavenly peace;

Sleep in heavenly peace.

JOSEPH MOHR; TRANSLATED BY JOHN F. YOUNG

Chapter Four

THE SHEPHERDS

The old woman continued. "I cleaned him and wrapped him up, then handed him to his mother, lying there on the hay. He was asleep soon enough—tired out, like we all were. He was born in the fourth watch of the morning.[1] I suppose I could have left then and they would have done fine. But I couldn't leave. I decided to stay and keep watch over them. The truth was I felt so good I didn't want it to end.

---

[1] In New Testament times, the night was divided according to Roman custom into four "watches," the fourth being approximately 2:30 A.M. until 5:00 A.M.

"I felt as though I were rejoicing over the birth of my own son. Yet, in fact, Mary and Joseph were strangers to me. Yes, I had grown close to them as one must, thrown together by fate into the grip of a birth. But, really, I didn't know them.

"Oh, of course, every birth is a miracle—a gift from God to rejoice in. But this was different, somehow, than all the others. Even as I felt it, I wondered, *Where is this intense feeling of joy and love coming from?*

"I looked around our little scene: I could not let go of the thought that everything around me was feeling the same thing. The goats and the donkey staring at us with their sleepy faces, the palm trees like proud giants assigned to stand guard, even the stars seeming to lean in from their places in heaven to get a closer look. I can't explain it. I only

know that I never felt such joy before or since. I wouldn't have changed places just then with the queen of Persia.

"'Isn't he wonderful, Hannah?' Mary said to me. 'What would I have done without you? You were an angel sent from God.'

"Well, I'm no angel. But I wondered if perhaps she was right about God sending me. Especially after Simon and his men arrived.

"Now this part of the story, Luke, you might have some difficulty believing. But I tell you, though more than thirty-five years have gone by since that night, I remember what happened next as if it were yesterday.

"All was quiet before the shepherds arrived. It was just before morning light, and Mary and Joseph had both fallen asleep. Maybe I had even dozed off.

"Voices seeped into my dreaming and woke me, and I heard the shuffling of footsteps. Suddenly I saw a man standing over me. It took me a moment to realize that it was Simon.

"Joseph was on his feet in an instant, his staff in his hand. For the second time that night he called out, 'Who's there?'

"'It's all right, Joseph,' I assured him. 'This man is Simon, our neighbor. What brings you here, Simon?'

"'Well . . .' he stammered '. . . the baby there. He brings me.'

"Then he turned and called down to some others on the path below.

"'I've found him! He's in here!'

"I felt for a moment I must still be dreaming. How could this baby have brought my neighbor?

"Suddenly there were four other men standing with Simon. Mary took the child from the bed we had made for him in the manger and held him close. I knew them all—hired hands of Simon, along with his young son, Daniel.

"They had the strangest looks on their faces, excited but solemn. Suddenly one of them went down on his knees, and one by one, so did all the others.

"'What on earth do you mean, Simon, that the baby brought you here? How did you even know there was a baby?'

"He looked at me like a man in a dream, and his voice was hushed. 'Because angels told us he was here, Hannah. We saw *angels*.'

"He fell silent and stared at his hands intently, his face wrinkling into a knotted frown. It wasn't an easy thing for a rough man like Simon to be telling me he had just spoken with an angel. But he felt that it was his place to speak for all of them, and so he continued.

"'There was a whole flock of angels! We were staying out in the fields. For the lambing. The light woke me. And there he was—a man, no, an angel, standing right there above me in a bright light. It nearly scared me out of my skin, Hannah. Nothing—no wolf, no bear—ever had me shaking like this sight. But the angel knew; he knew because he said to me, "Fear not! Fear not, for I bring you good news of great joy that shall be to all people!"'

"Simon gazed at the baby again and said, 'The angel said a Savior had been born in the city of David this very day, a Savior, the Anointed One of the Lord. Then the sky was filled with them! I saw it with my own eyes, Hannah. They were all praising God, and saying, "Glory to God in the highest, and on earth peace, good will toward men."'

"Simon's eyes filled with tears, and he said in a hushed voice, 'I'm only a shepherd, Hannah. I'm just a shepherd.'

"Just then his son Daniel burst out, 'You should've seen 'em! It was something! Amazing! There were hundreds of 'em!'

"At that, Daniel flung his arms up and out, as if to somehow demonstrate the immensity of the vision of God's glory. His words kept tumbling:

"'And then they told us where to find him! They said we'd find the baby wrapped in swaddling clothes and lying in a manger. And it's just like they told us!'

"Daniel did not seem to share his father's fear of the heralding angels. He accepted them as a matter of course

and saved his greatest excitement for the news they had brought. A wonderful baby had been born! Slowly, shyly, he moved as close as he could to Mary and her son and whispered, 'Can I touch him?'

"I looked into the faces of those humble men. I saw their tears and awe. How could I doubt their words? They had actually seen this amazing sight.

"And then I realized that Daniel was right—the most wonderful thing that night wasn't the heavenly host, as great as it must have been to see angels. The most wonderful thing was the baby. I caught my breath.

"Was this baby the very Messiah of God?

"Mary must have read my thoughts.

"'Yes, Hannah,' she said, 'it was promised to me. An angel told me that this child would be born to save his people. His name is to be Jesus—God saves.'[2]

"I looked at Joseph. He was nodding.

"I did not think my poor heart could take it in, but yet, I never questioned it. I knew I had heard the greatest news that any of us could ever hear. Our Savior, the hope of Israel, had finally come to us."

---

[2] Mary would have pronounced it "Yeshua"—the child's name in Aramaic.

Hark! the herald angels sing
Glory to the newborn King!
Peace on earth and mercy mild,
God and sinners reconciled!

CHARLES WESLEY

Chapter Five

THE PROMISE

Hannah breathed a deep sigh. She hoped this man Luke could feel a hundredth part of the wonder she felt each time she told the story.

She looked at him. He had listened very patiently but said nothing. He was Greek; could he understand what had happened that night so long ago?

Sensing her questions, Luke quickly spoke his reassurance. "Hannah, believe me, your story has more than met my hope; for Israel's hope is my hope also. What you have told me is exactly what I was seeking."

By nature as well as by his long years of training as a physician, Luke was a calm man in the face of any startling disclosure. Little did his face or his actions show what he might be thinking.

Yet Hannah instinctively trusted him. When he said he believed her, she knew he did. And that was enough.

Luke declined Hannah's offer to stay at the inn. He said this trip to Bethlehem, however glad he was that he had come, had put him behind schedule. He had pressing business in Jerusalem before embarking on another long journey, to Antioch in Syria. There he was joining companions to begin an even longer journey. The night of Jesus' birth had marked the beginning of a long, cascading chain of events that had changed the world for Hannah, for Luke, and for many others.

"I have put your story with the other stories I have gathered of Jesus, here, in my heart. I will remember everything you have told me, Hannah. I believe it is now my part to tell the story. There are so many people to tell."

She was somewhat startled by this revelation.

"How many people do you intend to tell, Luke?"

"The whole world, if I have the chance. I'm going to write it all down so the words can go to many more places than my own feet can carry me."

Hannah thought fast. A sudden vision presented itself of hundreds of pilgrims from Syria, from Macedonia, and from all the ends of the earth, coming to a little inn in Bethlehem of Judea to talk to the woman who had delivered the Messiah of men into the world. Suddenly her head ached. She felt herself to be an old woman.

"Luke. You may tell this story, of course. It does not belong to me. I have only one favor to ask. If you do tell the story—to the world, as you say—will you please leave me out of it? After all, it is not important who brought Him into this world, is it? Only that He came at all."

Luke considered this. He thought Hannah had gone a little pale.

"Don't worry, Hannah," he assured her. "You have my word that I will leave you out of my story entirely. It may be that among those who learn of the Messiah's birth there will be some who suspect the truth in their hearts—that someone must have been sent to help. But I will never tell them that the someone was the innkeeper's wife. I promise."

"Thank you, Luke," Hannah said. "I am content. I wish you Godspeed on your journey, and may the whole world indeed learn what you have to tell them."

Joy to the world, the Lord is come;

Let earth receive her King!

Let ev'ry heart prepare him room,

And Saints and angels sing.

Isaac Watts, altered by William W. Phelps

Lynda Wilson grew up in a military family and attended eleven different grade schools. It was then that books became her most constant friends. She has been writing since she was a child, recently completing a woman's scripture study of the book of Exodus. She is the founder of "Hugs across the Miles," an organization that has sent thousands of quilts and school supplies to orphanages in Russia and Jordan. The mother of four grown children, she and her husband live in Alamo, California.

Brandon Dorman was born and raised in University Place, Washington. His artistic career began in fourth grade when he was commissioned to draw images on his classmates' T-shirts. Ever since then Brandon has been in love with creating images. In 2005, he graduated from Brigham Young University–Idaho, where he studied Fine Art and Illustration. He recently moved back to Washington, with his wonderful wife and son, where he enjoys working as a freelance illustrator.